Fred J. Schonell
Phyllis Flowerdew

Oliver & Boyd

Acknowledgments

We are grateful to the following for supplying photographs and giving permission for their use: International Photobank, cover and p. 119; Combi Press Service, p. 118.

Illustrated by Moira Chesmur, Harry Horse, Peter Joyce, Maggie Ling, Caroline Sharpe and Patricia Tourret.

Oliver & Boyd
Longman House
Burnt Mill
Harlow
Essex CM20 2JE
An Imprint of Longman Group UK Ltd

First published 1950
Second edition 1965
Third edition 1976
Fourth edition 1985
Tenth impression 1993

ISBN 0 05 003749 8

Set in 14/20 pt 'Monophoto' Plantin
Produced by Longman Singapore Publishers Pte Ltd
Printed in Singapore

The publisher's policy is to use paper manufactured from sustainable forests.

Preface

The Wide Range Readers are planned to provide graded reading practice for junior school children. Because children of 7–11 have a wide range of reading needs and attainments, there are three parallel series—Blue, Green and Red books—to provide plenty of material to suit the interests and reading ages of every child.

Books 1–4 are graded by half yearly reading ages, for use by appropriate groups within a class. Book 1 should provide an easy read for children with a reading age of about 7–7½. Children with reading ages below 7 are recommended to use the Wide Range Starters.

The controlled vocabulary of the series makes the books suitable for the following reading ages:

6½–7	**Starter Books**—Blue, Green and Red
7–7½	**Book 1**—Blue, Green and Red
7½–8	**Book 2**—Blue, Green and Red
8–8½	**Book 3**—Blue, Green and Red
8½–9	**Book 4**—Blue, Green and Red
9+	**Book 5**—Blue, Green and Red
10+	**Book 6**—Blue, Green and Red
11+	**Book 7**—Red only
12+	**Book 8**—Red only

Where to Find the Stories

page

5 Moving Day for Ducks

15 The Red Bike

24 The Little Elephant who Couldn't Find his Tusks

34 Sandy the Sailor Dog

50 Working for a Wizard

60 The Hippo who Tried to Catch Cold

68 Lee's Little Sister

85 Seymour's Wish

92 The First Christmas

100 The Bogey-Cart

107 Peter and the Dyke

120 The Dancing Doll

Moving Day for Ducks

Once upon a time, not so long ago,
there were five baby ducks.
They were small and yellow and fluffy,
and they lived with their mother
beside a muddy patch of water in London.
All around were shops and houses,
tall and grey and ugly. All around
was the noise of wheels and engines.

"This is no place for baby ducks,"
said Mother Duck one morning.
"I know a park in London,
where there's a flowing river.
There are tall trees and green grass.
Come, little ducks. We'll move."

So the five baby ducks stood up
on the muddy bank,
and shook themselves. Moving was easy.
No tables and chairs and beds to take.
No clothes and shoes and toys to pack.
No windows to shut and doors to lock.
The five little ducks stood in a line
behind their mother,
and they all trotted away.

It was early in the morning,
and there was hardly anyone about.
Down the street trotted Mother Duck,
with the five baby ducks
close behind her.
Round corners, across roads,
past houses and shops they went.

At first they met only a cat
who had been out all night.
Then they met a dog who was having
an early morning walk.
Then they met a milkman
taking round milk, and a paper boy
slipping papers through the doors.

The cat stared. The dog stared.
The milkman stared. The boy stared.
But Mother Duck trotted on, and the
five baby ducks trotted on behind her.

It was not early morning now. People began to leave their homes and go to work. The roads were filled with cars, buses and vans. Everyone seemed to be in a hurry. No one had time to look at a mother duck and five fluffy, yellow baby ducks trotting along.

Only a girl on her way to school saw them Only a boy on a bicycle stopped to look. Only a big coal man on a coal cart shouted,

"Good morning, Mrs Duck. How's the family this morning?"

The baby ducks grew tired. Their feet were not used to hard streets. They had only walked on soft mud before.

"Are we nearly there?" they asked.

"Yes," said Mother Duck. "It's not far now. Keep close to me while we cross this street." Mother Duck and the five baby ducks

BLACK

stood in a line
on the edge of the street.
They were in a very busy part of London.
Cars, buses and vans rushed by.

"Wait a moment," said Mother Duck
to the five baby ducks. "You must
always be very careful when you
cross roads.
Find a safe place to cross, then stop.
Look all around for traffic,
then listen."

"Yes," said the five baby ducks.
They stopped and looked and listened.
They saw cars, buses and vans
rushing past. They looked
all around again. But still the cars,
buses and vans rushed past.

"We can't cross here,"
said Mother Duck at last. "Let's walk
a little further, and then try again."

Up the street trotted Mother Duck,
with the five baby ducks behind her.
Soon they saw a policeman standing
in the street, with cars,
buses and vans rushing past him.

"Ah!" said Mother Duck. "Here's
someone who'll help us."

Mother Duck and the five baby ducks
stood in a line
on the edge of the street.
They called out to the policeman,

"Please will you take us across the road?"

The policeman, of course,
thought they said,
"Quack, quack, quack,"
but he understood what they wanted
all the same.
He smiled and held out his arm.
The cars stopped. The buses stopped.
The vans stopped. There was a clear path
across the road.
Now it was safe to cross.

Mother Duck and the five baby ducks stepped into the road, and walked safely across to the other side.

Car drivers and bus drivers smiled at each other. Van drivers said,

"Just look at that."

People on the path stopped to look. A man took a picture to send to the newspaper.

Then the policeman put down his arms,

and the cars, buses and vans
rushed on again along the busy street.

But Mother Duck and the five baby ducks
had come to the park.
There they saw a flowing river,
tall trees and green grass.

For one moment they stood and stared,
because it was all so beautiful.
Then they gave little quacks of joy,
and splashed into the clear, cold water.

The Red Bike

Once upon a time there was
a boy called Andrew McAndrew.
The thing he wanted most was
a bike. Each night before he went
to sleep he said a little rhyme
to himself, which was a kind of wish.

"Andrew McAndrew, what would you like?
All I want is a little red bike."

But he never thought that anybody
heard him. On the morning of
his eighth birthday, his mother
woke him up.

"Happy birthday, Andrew," she said
and gave him a hug.
"Come downstairs for your birthday present."

Andrew ran downstairs and in the
hall he saw something all wrapped
in brown paper.

"What is it? What is it?" he said.
With a great ripping noise he
tore off the paper.

"Now you know what it is,"
said his mother. It was a bike—
a red bike just like the one
he had always wanted.
It had brakes. It had a white pump
to pump up the tyres.
And when the wheels went round
they made a loud whirring noise.
But best of all it had a
silvery bell which Andrew rang and rang.
Then he thanked his mum and dad
and went out to ride his bicycle.

Now Andrew McAndrew's grandad lived

just down the street.
The boy loved his grandad and he
wanted to show his new bike
to him before he did anything else.
But there was a sharp nail on
the road outside his grandad's gate.

Andrew didn't see it and
he rode right over it.
Suddenly there was
a loud bang and all the air
hissed out of his front tyre.

"Oh no," moaned Andrew.
He wanted to cry when he
saw his tyre was flat.
But instead of crying
he wished again with his rhyme.

"*Andrew McAndrew, what would you like?*
Somebody big to fix my bike."

Just then his grandad came out
of the gate. He had a
white moustache and a white beard.

"Happy birthday, Andrew," he said

with a big smile. Andrew
showed his grandad the bike and then
told him about the burst tyre.
He wanted to cry again.
His grandad patted him on the head
and said,

"Don't worry, I'll fix it for you."

His grandfather could fix anything.
He got his box of tools from
the kitchen, and a basin
full of water.
He took off the tyre and
showed Andrew the black rubber tube
inside it. Then he put the tube in
the basin of water
and a tiny line of bubbles
came out of the hole that
the nail had made.

"There's the trouble," said his grandad.
He cut a little patch from a
piece of old rubber and stuck it
over the hole with clear glue.

"That's it," he said. "Now all we have to do is pump it up again."
He began to pump up the tyre
with the brand new white pump.
Andrew saw the tyre get fat again.
His grandad pumped until the tyre
was like new.

"It's fixed now," said his grandad.
Now Andrew didn't feel like crying.
He showed off the brakes to his grandad.
He spun the wheels.
And best of all he let him listen
to the silvery bell which made a
grand noise.

"Goodbye," shouted Andrew. And he rode off down the road again.
As he cycled along he said a little rhyme.

"*Andrew McAndrew, what would you like*?
All my friends to see my bike."

And he went to call on all his friends, to show them his new bike.

Bernard MacLaverty

The Little Elephant who Couldn't Find his Tusks

Once upon a time there was
a little grey elephant who lived
in the great green forests of Africa.

One evening he went with his mother
down to the river to drink.
He went with his mother and three
other grown-up elephants.
He kept close beside them
and did what they did.

The big elephants dipped their trunks
into the river, and sucked up
the cool water.
So the little elephant dipped his trunk
into the river,
and sucked up the cool water.

The big elephants poured the water
into their wide open mouths.
So the little elephant poured the water
into his wide open mouth.

The big elephants stirred up the mud
with their big grey feet.
So the little elephant stirred
up the mud with his big grey feet.

The big elephants squirted water
at a floating log.
So the little elephant
squirted water at a floating log.

"I'm just like the big elephants,"
thought the little elephant.
"Everything they do, I can do.
Everything they have, I have."

Just then the sun began to set.
It sank low in the sky,
and turned the grey water of the river
to shining gold.
The big elephants watched the sun set.
So the little elephant
watched the sun set.

The big elephants went on
watching the sun set. But the little
elephant grew tired of watching it,
so he watched the big elephants instead.

"I'm just like the big elephants,"
thought the little elephant.
"They have one long, waving trunk each.
So have I. They have two big,
flapping ears each. So have I.
They have two white, shining
tusks each—"
He was just going to say, "So have I,"—
when he found that he hadn't.
He had no shiny white tusks at all.

"That's funny," thought the

little elephant. "They all
have shiny white tusks but me.
Where can mine be?
I must have lost them."

He opened his mouth to say
to his mother, "I've lost my tusks."
Then he thought, "She may say
I'm careless. She may tell me
to go and look for them.
Perhaps I'd better go a little way
and look for them first."

The little elephant stepped out
of the cool water and slipped away
between the trees.
He walked through the forest.
He looked to the east.
He looked to the west,
but he couldn't find his tusks.
He looked low in the grass.
He looked high in the trees,
but he couldn't find his tusks.

He saw a monkey

swing from a branch by his tail.

"It's time you went to bed," said the monkey.

"But I'm looking for something," said the little elephant.

"What have you lost?" asked the monkey.

"A pair of shiny, white tusks," said the little elephant. "Have you seen them?"

"No," said the monkey. "I haven't seen any tusks," and he jumped away through the trees, shouting,

"I haven't seen any tusks, any tusks, any tusks."

The little elephant walked on through the forest. He looked to the east. He looked to the west, but he couldn't find his tusks.

He saw a giraffe peeping over a tree.

"It's time you went to bed," said the giraffe.

“But I’m looking for something,” said the little elephant.

“What have you lost?” asked the giraffe.

“A pair of shiny, white tusks,” said the little elephant. “Have you seen them?”

“No,” said the giraffe, “I haven’t seen any tusks,” and he walked away, saying in a whisper,

"I haven't seen any tusks,
any tusks, any tusks."

The little elephant walked on through the forest.

He saw a lion lying beside a bush.

"It's time you went to bed," said the lion.

"But I'm looking for something," said the little elephant.

"What have you lost?" asked the lion.

"A pair of shiny, white tusks," said the little elephant. "Have you seen them?"

"No," said the lion. "I haven't seen any tusks," and he went prowling through the trees, roaring,
"I haven't seen any tusks,
any tusks, any tusks."

Now it was growing dark,
and the forest was full of shadows.
All the trees rustled their leaves.
All the leaves seemed to whisper,

"We haven't seen any tusks,
any tusks, any tusks."

"Oh, dear," said the little elephant
to himself, "I'll have to go back
and tell my mother
that I've lost my tusks.
I'll have to tell her
that I've looked to the east,
and looked to the west,
but I can't find my tusks.
I'll have to tell her
that I've looked low in the grass
and high in the trees,
and I *cannot* find my tusks."

So the little elephant went back
through the forest,
and came to his mother.

"I've lost my tusks,"
said the little elephant.
He thought his mother would say,
"How careless of you."
But she just looked at him, and said,

"Lost *what*?"

"My shiny, white tusks," said the little elephant. "I've looked everywhere, but I can't find them."

Then his mother lifted up her long, long trunk, and opened her great, wide mouth, and laughed. She laughed so loudly that all the trees shook with her laughing. Then she said,

"You haven't lost your tusks. You haven't had any yet. Babies are never born with teeth. Their teeth grow afterwards. Elephants are never born with tusks. Their tusks grow afterwards. When you are bigger, then your tusks will grow."

"Oh," said the little elephant, "I didn't know that. I thought I must have lost them."

By this time, it was dark, so he lay down beside his mother

and fell asleep. The stars came out,
and twinkled down
through the trees and bushes.
The moon came out, and shone
down on the little elephant.
It shone on his long trunk,
and his two big, flapping ears.
And it shone on two little knobs
at the side of his face.
These were his tusks,
just ready to start growing.

Sandy the Sailor Dog

Once upon a time there was a fisherman
who was in a hurry to go home to tea.
He pulled his boat up on the beach,
but not nearly as far up as usual.
He tied it to a post,
but not nearly as tightly as usual.
He left it there for the night.
He was in such a hurry
that he didn't see what a bad knot
he had tied in the rope.
It was a very bad knot,
and it began to slip
even as the fisherman walked away.
It slipped and slipped and slipped.

The sun sank down over the sea,
and it was evening.
Soon a little dog came that way.
He was a jolly little dog with a rough
coat the colour of sand,
and soft, brown eyes.

He was a stray dog
with no one to look after him,
and no warm bed to sleep in at night.
Often he was hungry,
and often he was cold and lonely.

He ran down the beach, leaving a row
of little paw marks in the sand.
He saw the boat tied to the post,
and he thought,

"Here's a good place to sleep."

So he jumped into it, and crept
under a seat. It was warm there,
and the wind couldn't reach him.

The little sandy dog thought how lucky
he was to find such a cosy bed.
But he didn't know
that the knot in the rope
was slipping, slipping, slipping.
He stretched his legs, closed his eyes
and fell asleep.

The sky and the sea grew dark,
and it was night.
Two tiny stars twinkled
and then hid themselves
behind a cloud.
The waves came splashing on to the sand,
nearer and nearer to the boat.

And the knot in the rope
was slipping, slipping, slipping.
The white foam shone in the darkness.
There was no sound
except the sound of the waves,
and the sigh of the little sleeping dog.

Nearer and nearer splashed the waves.
Nearer and nearer crept the white foam.
And all the time the knot in the rope
was slipping, slipping, slipping.

Then, just as the first wave
touched the boat, the knot came undone.
The rope slipped from the post
and slid down on the sand.
The boat began to sway and creak
as the water splashed up to it
and down again.
The little dog was warm and cosy.
He went on sleeping.

The waves came running
up the beach again.
They crept underneath the boat.

They splashed all round it.
They shook it and swayed it,
and pulled it and pushed it.
They carried it out to sea.

Out in the darkness sailed the boat,
all alone on the wide sea.
Out in the darkness sailed
the little sleeping dog, far away
from the beach, far away from the land,
up and down, up and down on the waves.

The little dog had a lovely dream.
He dreamt that he had a home of his own,
and kind people to look after him.
He dreamt that someone put down
a bowl of soup for him to drink,
and a big bone for him to eat.

Just then he awoke.
He felt strange, as if he were going up
and down, up and down.
For a moment he couldn't think
where he was. Then he thought,
"Ah yes! A nice warm, cosy boat."

But oh! The boat was moving.
It was tossing up and down.
It was sailing out to sea!

The little dog jumped to his feet.
Perhaps he hadn't sailed far.
Perhaps he could jump ashore.
Perhaps he could swim to land.
But the moon came out
to show him that he could not.
It made a silver path in front of him,
to show him how wide and dark
the sea was.

The little dog was frightened.
He barked as loudly as he could.
He ran from one end of the boat
to the other, and back again,
and back again, and back again.
He barked and barked
but there was no one to hear him.
No fish put up its head to listen.
No ship was near enough to hear,
and land was far, far away.

At last the little dog was too tired to bark any more. Sadly he crept under the seat again, and stretched his legs as he lay down to sleep. What would happen to him now? He didn't know. The waves rocked him, and the sea sang sleepy songs to him.

He closed his eyes once more,
and soon he was fast asleep.

All night long
the boat tossed up and down.
All night long the little sleeping dog
sailed on the wide dark sea.

When he awoke next time, it was morning,
and the sky was pink with the rising sun.
The little dog blinked his eyes
and stood up in the boat.
He shook himself
from the tip of his cold black nose
to the end of his sandy tail.
He stretched himself, first his front legs,
then his back legs.
He was used to tossing up and down
on the waves now, and he felt
much better. On to a seat he jumped,
and there he stood, gazing all round.
He saw only blue sky and blue sea.
He didn't see a ship, or a bird,
or any land.

For a moment he felt sad and lonely again. Then he said to himself,

"Something is sure to happen soon."

But it didn't. All through the day the boat sailed, but it came no nearer to land. All the next night it tossed up and down on the waves, and all the next day it drifted and drifted on the wide blue sea. By that time the little dog was hungry. He had often been hungry before, because he was a stray dog with no home of his own, but he had never been as hungry as this!

That evening there was a beautiful sunset. All the sky and all the sea seemed to be painted pink and gold. The waves sparkled and danced and the clouds were like silver. It was so beautiful that even the poor, tired, hungry little dog had to climb on the seat to look.

And as he looked he saw something
which seemed more beautiful to him
than the sunset.
He saw funnels—
two fat, grey funnels
puffing smoke up into the evening sky.
A ship! A ship!
And it was coming this way!
The little dog gave three small barks.
The first was a wuff of surprise.
The second was a yelp of joy.
The third was a call for help.
And then he barked and barked
as loudly as he could.
Oh, how he barked!
He ran from one end of the boat
to the other, and back again,
and back again, and back again.
He stood on each seat in turn,
and stretched himself as high
as he could.
He barked and barked.

Would any one on the ship see him?
Would any one hear him?
Would the ship stop?
Would he be saved after all,
or left to float all night again
on the wide, dark sea?

Now at this moment, on the ship,
a sailor who was keeping watch,
was looking through a telescope.
At first he saw only sky and sea.
Then he saw something brown
floating on the water.

"Just a bit of wood," he thought.
He moved the telescope,
so that he could see more clearly.
He saw that it wasn't a bit of wood.
It was a little boat, an empty boat,
which had somehow become lost.

"There's an empty fishing boat
over there," he told the nearest sailor,
and that sailor went to the captain.

"There's an empty fishing boat
over there," he said.

The captain went quickly

to the sailor on watch.

"Are you sure there's no one in it?" he asked.

"Yes," said the sailor, looking through the telescope. "I can't see anyone." Then he shouted in surprise, "There *is* someone in it, someone very small, who keeps moving about. It looks like—a dog!"

A little later the ship steamed up close to the fishing boat. Its fat, grey funnels sent puffs of smoke up into the pink and gold sky. Oh, how pleased the little dog was! Sailors came to the rails and leaned over, and whistled to him. They shouted,

"All right, little dog, we'll soon save you."

The little sandy dog barked and barked with joy and excitement.

Now the ship came very near, and made great waves that almost upset the little boat.

A rope ladder was let down
from the deck, and a sailor climbed
down it. He climbed down and down,
till he swung right over the fishing boat.
Then he leaned forward,
and lifted up the little dog.

After that, so many nice things
happened, that the little sandy dog
thought he must be dreaming.
One sailor gave him a bowl of bread
and milk, and another gave him
a dish of hot soup. One gave him
a lump of sugar,
and another gave him a big bone.
Everyone patted him and stroked him,
and said what a brave dog he was.
The little dog was *so* pleased.
He jumped up at each sailor in turn.
He licked one, and cuddled up
against another. He wagged his tail
so hard that it was a wonder
he didn't wag it off.

Then one sailor said,
"I must go to bed because I'm on watch early in the morning.
Coming with me, Sandy?"
The little dog cocked up one ear, and thought, "He must mean me. My name must be Sandy."
He followed the sailor into his cabin.
There, because he was so tired, he curled up on the end of the bed, with his sandy tail over his little black nose, and fell asleep.

He was cosy and happy,
and warm and safe at last.

And what happened then?
Can you guess?

Well, Sandy stayed on the ship
and became a real sailor dog.
There was plenty of food
for him to eat.
There were a hundred sailors
to make him happy, from the captain
to the little cabin boy.

So Sandy sails round the world.
He sees strange lands and waving
palm trees. He hears seagulls cry,
and monkeys chatter.
He sees people from all over
the world—Africa, India and China.
He visits hot lands and cold lands.
He sails calm seas and stormy seas,
and he is as happy
as any little dog could be!

Working for a Wizard

Once upon a time there was a boy
named Robbie, who worked for a wizard.
Sometimes he worked hard
and did everything well.
Sometimes he didn't work hard,
and sometimes, just sometimes,
he was very, very lazy.

One day the wizard said,
"I'm going out this morning.
I want you to scrub the floor
while I'm away."

He went out and shut the door,
and Robbie was left alone.

"I don't want to scrub the floor,"
he thought. You see, this was one
of the days when he was lazy, very lazy.
He looked at the broom
standing in the corner. He looked out
of the window at the well,
which was at the end of the garden.

"I'll have to walk all the way
to the well to fetch water,"
he thought.
Then he said, "I know! I'll make
the broom do the work."

He knew a little of the wizard's magic,
so he whispered some magic words
to the broom. Then he said loudly,

"Broom, fetch some water from the well."

In a second the broom
grew two little legs and two little arms.
It walked out of the room,
and down the garden.
In another second it came back,
carrying two pails of water.

"Good!" thought Robbie.

The broom tipped up the pails,
and emptied the water on the floor.
Clang went the pails.
Splash went the water.
Then out of the door,
and down to the well
went the broom.

In a second, back came the broom
with two more pails of water.
It tipped up the pails,
and emptied the water on the floor.
Clang went the pails.
Splash went the water.

"That's fine!" said Robbie.
"That will be enough, thank you."

But the broom went out of the door
again, and down to the well.
Back it came
with two more pails of water.

"No more. No more," cried Robbie.
"Take those two back."

But the broom emptied the water
on the floor. Clang went the pails.
Splash went the water,
and out went the broom to get more.

"Stop, stop!" cried Robbie,
but the broom didn't stop.
Robbie didn't know the magic words
that would make it stop.

On went the broom, in and out,
in and out. Clang went the pails.
Splash went the water.

Robbie didn't know what to do.
Soon the room would look like a pond.
Soon the water would reach the shelves
where the wizard kept his magic powders.
Then what would happen?

On went the broom, in and out, in and out. Clang went the pails. Splash went the water.

"I'll *make* you stop!" shouted Robbie angrily. He rushed at the broom. He lifted it up and banged it against the wall with all his might. Crash! The broomstick broke into twenty pieces.

"Good," said Robbie. "Now you'll have to stop."

But did it stop? Oh, no! The twenty pieces became twenty tiny brooms. The twenty tiny brooms grew little arms and legs. Each tiny broom held two pails. So now there were twenty brooms going in and out, in and out, with pails of water. There were twenty brooms

tipping up the pails
and pouring the water on the floor.

In and out, in and out
went the twenty brooms.
Clang went the pails.
Splash went the water.

"Oh, dear!" cried Robbie.
"*Now* what can I do?"

He jumped on a chair,
to keep out of the way of the water.
The water rose higher and higher.
Robbie climbed on the table.

In and out, in and out
went the twenty brooms.
Clang, clang, clang went the pails.
Splash, splash, splash went the water.

Suddenly the wizard came back.
For a moment he stared at the water
and at the brooms,
and at Robbie up on the table.
Then he gave a loud shout of anger,
and a low whisper of magic.

At once the twenty brooms
turned back into one broom.
Arms and legs and pails were gone.
There was only lazy little Robbie
in the middle of the table,
and a pool of water
flowing out through
the door.

"Now," said the wizard, "clear up the room and scrub the floor."

Sadly Robbie climbed down from the table. Sadly he took the broom and began to scrub.
His very, very lazy day was over, and I think it was the last of his lazy days, don't you?

Adapted

The Hippo who Tried to Catch Cold

Once there was a small hippopotamus
who wanted a handkerchief. He wanted one
more than anything else in the world.

He asked his mother for one but
she said, "Don't be silly. What do you need
a hanky for? You haven't got a cold."

Little hippo thought about this
for a while. Then he said to himself,

"I'd better try to catch a cold
and then maybe I can have
a handkerchief."

But he didn't know how to catch
a cold. So he went to the park
to think about it. He lay down
on the grass and soon he
fell fast asleep. When he woke up
some people were standing staring at him.

"I shouldn't lie there if I were you,"
said an old lady kindly.

"The grass is damp and you might catch cold."

"Goody!" said little hippo.

"What's good about catching cold?" asked Tom the postman.

"Well, then I can have a handkerchief," explained little hippo.

Some children laughed. "You don't need a cold to have a handkerchief," said a girl called Ann.

"I do," said hippo sadly. "My mother can't think of any other reason for having one. Can you?"

"Well you *might* need one to collect conkers in," suggested Ann. And she took a green handkerchief out of her pocket and held each corner together so that it made a little bag.

"Or to make a sun-hat on a very hot day," said Tom the postman. And he took out a big checked handkerchief and knotted the corners. Then he took off his postman's cap and put on the handkerchief sun-hat.

"Or to bandage your foot if you had an accident," said Sue the nurse. And she folded her very clean white handkerchief to make a bandage.

"Or to dry your eyes if you hear a sad story and it makes you cry a little bit," said the old lady. And she took out a lavender-coloured hanky with a lace edge and dabbed her eyes.

"Or to find out which way the wind is blowing," said Jack the sailor. And he took out a large blue handkerchief and held it up in the air. "It's a west wind today," he said.

"Or to make a toy rabbit," said Ann's brother Michael. And he

folded his grey handkerchief round his fingers
into the shape of a rabbit.

"Or to make a flag to fly
if the Queen or anyone important comes,"
said Michael's friend, Ali.
And he took out an orange handkerchief
and knotted the two corners to a stick.

Little hippo smiled.

"So a handkerchief really *would* be very useful even if I *didn't*
catch a cold?" he said.

"Yes," everyone agreed.
Then Michael said,

"Here, you can have mine," and he
gave little hippo the grey rabbit handkerchief.

"And mine," said Ann, handing him
the green hanky.

"And mine," said Tom the postman,
taking the knotted hanky sun-hat off his head.

One by one they all gave little hippo
their handkerchiefs.

"Oh, *thank* you," said little hippo,
and he was so pleased
he turned head over heels
on the grass. Then he ran home to
show them all to his mother.

"Mother!" he called. "Look at—at—at—
ATISHOO!" And little hippo
sneezed loudly.

"Dear me," his mother said.

"You've caught a cold! How lucky that
I've just been to buy you a handkerchief."
She gave little hippo a huge
brown hanky and he
sneezed into it three times:

"ATISHOO! ATISHOO! ATISHOO!"

"I'll keep this one for colds,"
said little hippo snuffily,
"and the others for other things.
You know, Mother, handkerchiefs can be
such useful things . . . a—a—a ATISHOO!"

Daphne Lister

Lee's Little Sister

As soon as the bell rang,
Lee and his friends ran out of school.
They raced down the playground
to see who would be first
out of the gate.

Lee thumped his friend Alan
with his schoolbag.

"See you in the park," he shouted.
"All right," yelled Alan.
"Last one there's the goalkeeper!"
Lee stuffed his bag under
his anorak. He raced down the road
bumping into the other children
as they walked home.
He tripped over Sharon and
her friend who were sitting on
the low wall swopping photo-cards.
"Big banana feet!" yelled Sharon.
But Lee was in too much of
a hurry to stop and shout back.

He turned the corner into the road where he lived. His house was three along from the end. Lee stopped by the pillarbox and watched. His mum was not in the garden or at any of the windows. Very quietly he walked up the path, opened the door and pushed his bag into the hall. He turned to walk round the side of the house.

"Lee, is that you?" his mum shouted from the kitchen. "Where are you off to? I want you to take your little sister to the park with you."

"Oh Mum, not again!" moaned Lee, kicking the path.

"Yes," said his mum, coming to the door. "She can go with you and the boys. Keep an eye on her, will you?"

"Lin's a pest!" said Lee.

"She's your little sister," said his mum. "Either you take her or you don't go."

"Well, hurry up then," said Lee. "The others will all be there by now. I'll be left to play goalie again."

He had to stand and wait while his mum helped Lin into her anorak. Lin put her arms into the wrong sleeves and finished up with the hood over her face.

"Oh hurry up!" shouted Lee, jumping up and down on the path.

"She's only four!" said his mum.

Lee grabbed Lin's hand and started to run round to the back of the house. There was a hedge at the bottom of the back garden. The park was on the other side of the hedge.

"Don't go that way," shouted his mum. "You know your dad is trying to get that hedge to grow thicker."

Lee had to run back round the house, out of the front gate and all the way round to the park gates. Lin ran along beside him.

"You're a pest," said Lee, "a real pest!" Lin smiled.

In the park, the others were kicking the ball about on the grass.

"Hurry up," they shouted. Lee ran over to join them and Lin began to cry.

"I want to go on the swings,"
she cried. "You have to push me."

The boys kicked the ball about.
Lin went on crying.

"It's no use," said Lee.
"We'll have to put her on the swings.
My mum will hear her if we don't."

"Your sister is a real pest,"
said Alan. They put her on
a swing and all the boys
took turns at pushing.

"Higher," shouted Lin, laughing. "Push me higher."

At last Lee stopped.

"We're going to play football now," he said. "You'll have to play on your own for a while."

"I want to play football too!" shouted Lin. She started to cry again so they had to let her kick around for a bit. At last Lin went off to play on the climbing frame.

"Right," said the boys. "Let's have a game. You're goalkeeper, Lee. Last one here's always goalie!"

Lee stood between the two anoraks that marked his goal posts. He watched the ball carefully, jumping backwards and forwards to see where it was.

The striker for the other team

raced up the field towards him. He ran past most of Lee's team. Alan fell over his feet trying to stop him.

"Get him, Lee!" the boys in his team shouted.

Just then there was a cry from the top of the climbing frame.

"I'm stuck," shouted Lin. "I'm stuck!" Lee turned to see what had happened and the ball went past him through the goal.

"Oh no!" yelled Alan and the others.

"Not my fault," shouted Lee, kicking it back. They stood and watched as Lin came back down the climbing frame.

"I did it myself!" she shouted, jumping up and down on the grass. "I did it myself!"

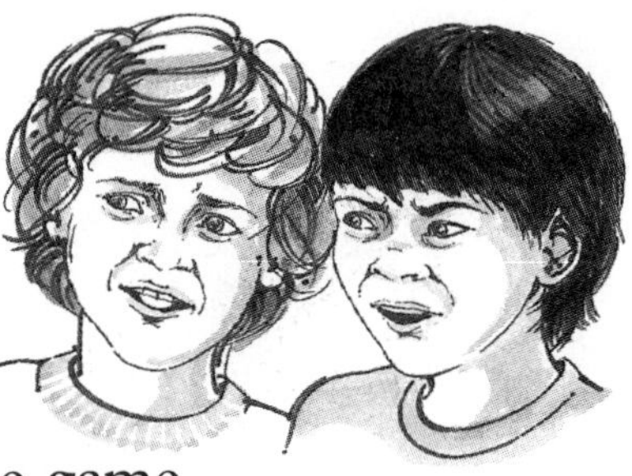

"Your little sister is a Super Pest," said Alan.

"You're telling me!" said Lee.

In the second half of the game Alan gave one huge kick. The ball went flying high over the fence and into a garden on the other side of the park.

"Now you've done it," said Lee. "That's Granny Green's. She'll never give it back to us. She says we're always trying to pinch her fruit." They stood in a row looking through the fence.

The ball lay right in the
middle of Granny Green's lawn,
just where she could see it
from the house.

"If we could sneak through the fence
we could get it back ourselves,"
said Lee.

"We're all too big!" said Alan.

Lin came over to see what had happened. She stood and looked through the fence. Then, before they could stop her, she slipped through between the posts.

"Hey!" shouted Lee. "Come back!" Lin ran across the grass and picked up the ball. Just then, Granny Green came out of the house.

The boys watched in horror as
she took Lin's hand and
led her into the house.
They stood by the fence and
waited for her to come back out again.
They waited for a long time.

"Do you think she's going to keep
your little sister?" whispered Alan.

"Oh no, she won't do that,"
said Lee, but he was worried.
There was no sign of Lin coming
back out.

"Maybe we should tell the police
she's been kidnapped!"
said one of the other boys.
"There was a story in my comic
last week just like that!"

"Rubbish!" said Alan. But he
wasn't too sure either.

Suddenly a voice shouted "Coo-ee"
from across the park. They all
turned to see Lin standing at the gate.

She was holding Granny Green's hand.
In her other hand she was
holding a big plastic bag.

"Goodbye," called Granny Green,
dropping their ball on the grass.
She gave it a kick and
sent it rolling towards the boys.

"Bye," shouted Lin. She ran across
to the boys.

"What's in the bag?" they asked,
crowding around.

Lin opened the plastic bag.
It was full of beautiful soft pink plums.

"There are too many on the tree," said Lin. "Granny Green gave them to us."

The boys decided there and then to call the game a draw.
They sat on the swings and ate the plums.

"You know," said Alan. "Your sister isn't really such a pest.
Maybe she should come and play with us again."

Lee nodded. He couldn't say anything because his mouth was full of sweet juicy plum.

Moira Miller

Seymour's Wish

Seymour loved tomato sauce. Every time he sat down for his tea, he reached for the bottle of tomato sauce and poured it over his food.

Slurp! slurp! slurp! it went.

Macaroni cheese—and tomato sauce.
Bangers and mash—and tomato sauce.
Fish and chips—and *lots* of tomato sauce!

Slurp! slurp! slurp!

“I love tomato sauce!” said Seymour, smacking his lips and pouring more sauce on his plate.

A bottle of tomato sauce didn’t last very long in Seymour’s house.

One night, Seymour was in his bed when he saw the moon peeping through the curtain at him.

“Hello Moon. Do you like tomato sauce? I do. I wish everything tasted of tomato sauce.”

And the moon winked at him.

The next morning, Seymour came running downstairs for his breakfast.
He sat down at the table,
poured milk on his cornflakes and
took a big spoonful.

"Mmmmmm! Tomato sauce!
My cornflakes taste of tomato sauce!"

And he finished off the plateful
in no time at all.
Then he spread marmalade on his toast
and took a big bite.

"Mmmmmm! Tomato sauce! That toast tastes of tomato sauce too! Yum yum!"

So he spread himself another slice.

At eleven o'clock, he came in
from the garden for his orange juice
and guess what! It tasted
of tomato sauce too!
Seymour was a bit surprised.

At lunchtime, he didn't mind that his toasted cheese tasted of tomato sauce,
because he normally liked tomato sauce

on it. But when his apple
tasted like that too, he wasn't
very happy. He liked the taste
of apples and he was beginning
to get tired of tomato sauce.

But he really was upset that afternoon
when his grandfather bought him
a great big ice-cream cone and
he took a long lick of it.
Yes, it tasted of tomato sauce too!

"Oh no! Not tomato sauce.
And I *like* ice-cream."

Tea-time wasn't much better.
Everything he ate tasted of tomato sauce.
Even the bread and butter pudding with
all the juicy raisins in it,
and the cup of cocoa he had
before going to bed tasted of
nothing but tomato sauce.
Seymour was tired of tomato sauce.

"Oh dear, I'm beginning not to like
tomato sauce *at all*."

ICE-CREAM
MILK

That night in bed, Seymour waited for the moon to appear. As soon as he saw him peeping through the curtain, Seymour said,

"Oh, Mr Moon, can't you help? Everything I eat tastes of tomato sauce."

"But that's what you wished for," said Mr Moon.

"I know, but I don't like it now.
It's so boring. Everything tastes the same."

"Ah yes," said Mr Moon wisely. "You've
had too much of a good thing.
Well, tomorrow everything will be
as it used to be. But from now on
be careful what you wish for."

"Oh thank you, Mr Moon," said Seymour.

Sure enough, the next day cornflakes tasted
like cornflakes, and pudding like pudding,
and best of all, ice-cream like ice-cream.

"Thank goodness," said Seymour at tea-time
as he reached for the bottle of
tomato sauce to pour on his
fish fingers.

But this time, he just put
a little slurp of the sauce
on his plate.

"After all," he said to himself,
"you can have too much of a good thing."

Ann R. Burnett

The First Christmas

It was evening in Bethlehem.
Mary and Joseph were very tired,
for they had come a long way.
"Here's an inn," said Joseph.
"Let's knock at the door,
and ask if we can stay for the night."
So Mary and Joseph walked up the
path, and knocked at the door.
"Please," said Joseph to the innkeeper,
"have you a bed for us tonight?"

"I'm sorry," said the innkeeper.
"There's no room in the inn.
There are so many people
in Bethlehem tonight."

So Mary and Joseph walked
down the path again.

"Never mind," said Joseph gently.
"We'll find another inn."

Soon they came to another inn.
They walked up the path
and knocked at the door.

"Please," said Joseph to the innkeeper,
"have you a bed for us tonight?"

"I'm sorry," said the innkeeper.
"There's no room in the inn.
There are so many people
in Bethlehem tonight."

Sadly Mary and Joseph walked
down the path again.

"Never mind," said Joseph.
"Here are some houses. Perhaps
one of these will have a bed to spare."

So Mary and Joseph
knocked at one house, then at another,
and then at another, but at
every house the answer was the same,
"I'm sorry. I've no beds to spare.
There are so many people
in Bethlehem tonight."
At last they came to another inn.
"Surely this one will have room for us,"
said Mary.
They walked up the path
and knocked at the door.
"Please," said Joseph,
"have you a bed for us tonight?"
"I'm sorry," said the innkeeper,
just as the others had said.
"There's no room in the inn.
There are so many people
in Bethlehem tonight."
"Oh," said Mary. She said it softly,
and no one heard. She was tired.
She didn't know how she could

walk another step. She was tired, so tired.
"Never mind," whispered Joseph.
He put his arm round her, and helped her slowly down the path, but the innkeeper didn't close the door.
He felt sorry for them
because they looked so sad.
They must have come a long way.
They looked tired, so tired.
"Just a moment," said the innkeeper.
"I haven't a bed for you,
but if you like, you may sleep
in the stable at the side of my inn.
It's large and dry, and only part of it
is used for my animals. I can give you
fresh straw to lie on, and I can lend
you blankets and a lantern."
Joseph looked at Mary.
"Shall we sleep in the stable, Mary?"
he asked her.
"Yes," said Mary. "Even a stable
will be better than nothing."

So the innkeeper led them to the stable.
He put a great pile of fresh straw
upon the floor, and he brought food
and blankets and a lantern.
Then he closed the door, and went away.

Mary and Joseph had their supper,
and then lay down on the straw to rest.
It was so nice to lie down at last,
and the straw made a bed
as soft as a cloud.

At one end of the stable were horses
and cows, and one or two sheep,
and a little grey donkey.
They were very quiet, as if they
knew that Mary and Joseph were tired.
They only blinked a little,
and gazed with big, gentle eyes.
The lantern made a pool of yellow light
on the floor, and sent shadows dancing
on the stable walls.

So Mary and Joseph slept in the stable.

And in the middle of the night
when all was dark and still,
God sent a present to them.
He sent a little baby boy, Baby Jesus.
Mary took Him in her arms,
and wrapped Him in a blanket.

"Where shall the Baby sleep?"
she asked.
Joseph turned up the lantern light,
and said,

"See, there's an empty manger. It's just the right size for a cradle."

So they put fresh straw in the manger,
and they laid Baby Jesus
gently down in His strange cradle.
The horses, the cows, the sheep
and the little grey donkey gazed at Him
with their big, gentle eyes.
The lantern made a pool of yellow light
on the floor, and sent shadows
dancing on the stable walls.

And outside, above the stable roof,
shone a star—large and clear,
bright and gleaming—
a star for Baby Jesus,
the new little King.

The Bogey-Cart

Andrew McAndrew sat on his front doorstep
watching a creepy-crawly.
It had so many legs—
hundreds and hundreds—and they rippled
as it moved along. They moved
the same way as the teeth of a comb
move when you run your thumb
across them. When the creepy-crawly
went away Andrew McAndrew was bored.

When Andrew McAndrew wanted anything badly
e said a little rhyme and
ery often he got his wish.
o he said,

"*I wish, I wish I'd something to do.*
Go to Grandad. Maybe he's bored too."

So Andrew McAndrew went to see his grandad
who stayed down the street from him.
His grandad had lots of interesting
things that Andrew liked to play with.
He had a box full of
buttons and screws and marbles and
things that he couldn't think of a use for.
There was a little shed where
his grandad worked, which had a
squeaky door.

"Hello Grandad," said Andrew
opening the door.

"Well, if it isn't Andrew,"
said his grandad. He was bending over
something lying on the floor.
There was a great sound of hammering

and banging. His grandad stopped working
and spoke to him.

"Well now, what do you think I'm making?"
Andrew looked and saw a board with
a little seat on it.
At the back and at the front
were two metal rods. He said to himself,

"*I hope, I hope with all my heart*
Grandad is building a bogey-cart."
Then he said out loud,

"I think it's a bogey-cart."

"A bogey-cart! Full marks.
That's what it is."
Andrew jumped up and down and yelled.

"Don't get so excited Andrew,"
said his grandad. "It's not finished yet.
What do we need to finish it?"

Andrew looked at the cart and
thought of the creepy-crawly's legs.

"Something it can go on,"
he said. "Wheels."

"That's right," said his grandad.

"You come with me and we'll find
something to make it go."

His grandad took him out of
the garden shed and they walked down
the road to the scrap-yard.
There were lots of old cars
and prams and washing machines
piled on top of one another.
His grandad knew the man who owned
the scrap-yard. His grandad seemed to
know everybody.

"Now," he said, "the man says
we can have anything we want
to make our bogey-cart."

Andrew and his grandad
walked round the scrap-yard
looking at the piles of rubbish. Suddenly
Andrew noticed a battered old pram.

"Look, Grandad," he said.
"There's an old pram. Could you
take the wheels off it and fix them
on to the cart?"

"Oh yes," said his grandad, "I can easily do that." His grandad could fix anything.

So they took the pram wheels back to his grandad's shed. The door squeaked as they opened it. Then his grandad hammered and thumped and thumped and hammered.

At last the bogey-cart was ready. It had two wheels at the back and two wheels at the front. The front wheels could be steered left or right by pulling on a piece of rope which was tied to the ends of the axle. The axle was fastened to the bogey-cart by a large nut and bolt which allowed it to move freely.

The cart was upside down and Andrew spun the wheels.

"That's an awful noise," said his grandad. "What they need is a drop of oil."

He got his little oil-can with the long thin spout and squeezed it into the noisy part of the wheels. The oil-can made a clicking sound, then the oil came out. Andrew spun the wheels again and this time the squeaking went away.

"Now it's ready for the road," said his grandfather.

Andrew McAndrew got into the seat of

the bogey-cart and his grandad puffed and puffed as he pushed the cart to the top of the hill.

"I'm too old for this," he said and he stood up and put his hand to his back. But Andrew was away. Steering the wheels with the rope, he said a little rhyme to himself,

"*Andrew McAndrew, how great it feels*
To be whizzing down a hill on wheels."

Bernard MacLaverty

Peter and the Dyke

The sails of the windmill turned round
and round. Peter watched them
as he walked slowly along the road
to school. He was early,
so there was no need to hurry.
There was time to watch the windmill.
There was time to listen to the sea.

Peter lived long ago, in Holland
where the fields were flat and low.
They were so low that sometimes
the sea had come rushing over them.
So the people had built high walls
or dykes to keep the sea away.
The dykes were very big and strong,
and though the sea splashed
up against them, it could
not get past them.
So the fields, the houses,
the people and the animals
were kept safe and dry.

This morning the sea was very rough, for Peter could hear the waves roaring against the dyke. Crash went the waves.

"It's no good," said Peter. "You can't get in." Crash, crash went the waves.

"It's no good," said Peter again. "You *can't* get in."

Then he saw two of his friends a little way ahead. They were running and laughing,

and throwing a ball to each other.
"Hello!" shouted Peter. "Wait for me."
He put his hand in his pocket,
to keep his lunch apple
from jumping about.
Then he ran and caught up
with the other boys.
The sails of the windmill
went on turning in the sun,
and the waves of the sea
went on crashing against the dyke.

The day at school passed very quickly.
Soon it was afternoon
and Peter was on his way home again.
His friends had already gone,
for Peter had stayed late
to tidy up the classroom.
He liked helping, but he felt
a bit lonely walking home on his own.
There was no one else on the road
at all. The sails of the windmill
were turning again in the sun,
and the waves of the sea
were crashing again on the dyke.

Crash, crash went the waves.

"The noise is very loud today,"
thought Peter. "What a good thing
the dykes are thick and strong."

Then he forgot about the sea,
and began to wonder if his mother
had baked any cakes today.
She made such nice cakes, big ones
and small ones, currant buns

and sticky jam tarts. Peter felt hungry
at the thought of them,
and he began to walk more quickly.

But what was that queer little noise?
He stopped and listened.
It wasn't the sound of the windmill
creaking. It wasn't the sound
of the sea against the dyke.
It was a new sound,
a queer little trickling noise.
What could it be?
Peter looked all round.
At first he couldn't see anything.
Then he saw a thin silvery line
on the dyke.
He knelt down to look at it.

There was a hole, a tiny hole,
and the sea was trickling through it,
and running down on to the road
like a baby river.

A hole in the dyke!
Quickly Peter hunted along the road

till he found a stone.
He pushed it into the hole, and waited
to see if it would be any good.
It stuck for a moment,
and then came out with the water.
It needed more than a stone
to keep back the trickle of sea.

Peter knew what would happen.
The trickle would grow to the size
of a stream. The stream would grow
to the size of a river.
Then the dyke would crumble and break,
and the wild sea would come
sweeping over the land.
Fields and houses would be washed away.
People and animals would be drowned.

"I must run for help," said Peter
to himself. "I must find someone
to mend the dyke
before the hole gets any bigger."
He was just about to run home
when he thought of something else.

By the time he had brought someone back
to mend the dyke, it might be too late.
He knelt down again to look at the hole.
It was bigger already.
Peter closed his fingers,
and put his hand into the hole.
It just fitted.
The trickle of water stopped.

"My hand is just the right size," thought the little boy. "I'd better stay here till someone comes along."
So there he knelt
with his fist in the hole.
The sails of the windmill turned
round and round, and the waves of the sea went on crashing against the dyke.

"You can't get in," said Peter.

Crash, crash went the waves.

"It's no good," said Peter. "You can't get in—as long as I stay here."

Someone would be sure to come
along the road in a moment.
But no one came.
Peter's hand grew very cold.
The sun began to sink behind the trees.
It would soon be dark. Someone would be sure to come along in a moment.

But no one came.
The sun slipped out of sight.
Darkness hid the fields.

The windmill was silent.
It held its sails to the sky
like great black arms,
and still Peter knelt on the roadside,
with his hand pressed into the hole.
The waves crashed and roared against
the dyke. Peter's hand was cold as ice,
but he didn't take it away. If he took
his hand away, the hole would get bigger.
The trickle of water would grow
to the size of a stream. The stream
would grow to the size of a river.
Then the dyke would crumble and break,
and the wild sea would come
sweeping over the land.
Fields and houses would be washed away.
People and animals would be drowned.
He *must* keep his hand there. Someone
would be sure to come along soon.

But still no one came. Then Peter knew
that no one would come now.
He would have to stay there

all through the night. He was tired,
and very, very sleepy.
He was cold, very cold,
and his hand was like ice.
Slowly his head went forward
and his eyes began to close.
He jerked his head up again,
and opened his eyes wide.

"I mustn't go to sleep," he thought,
"in case my hand slips out of the hole.
I mustn't go to sleep."

Crash, crash went the waves
against the dyke.

"You can't come in," whispered Peter.
"I won't let you in. I won't *let* you in."

And he didn't.
All through the night he knelt there
—stiff and cold and hungry and tired.
All through the night he kept his hand
pressed into the hole in the dyke.
All through the night
he kept back the wild sea.

At last morning came. The sun peeped out above the trees. The sails of the windmill began to turn again. Two men walked along the road on their way to work, and there they found Peter, brave little Peter, with his hand still in the hole in the dyke.

So the dyke was mended,
and Peter was carried home to bed.
The sails of the windmill
went on turning in the sun,
and the waves of the sea
went on crashing against the dyke.

Adapted

On the left is a statue of Peter. It stands in the Dutch town of Spaarndam. Peter has his hand in the hole in the dyke and is looking round to see if anyone is coming to help him.

Above, you can see two old Dutch windmills standing by a canal. The land behind the windmills is below the level of the sea and special care must be taken to keep it safe and dry.

The Dancing Doll

Long, long ago in France, lived a wise man.
He was very clever and he made
things that no one had ever made before.
One day he took some wood and a knife,
and he began to carve a doll.
He said to himself,
"This will be a wonderful doll.
When I've carved her from wood, I'll
make a tiny machine to put inside her.
The machine will help her to move
her arms and her legs, so that

she'll be able to walk and dance,
just like a real little girl."

So the wise man worked at the doll
day after day, week after week.
He carved out her head and body,
her arms and legs. He built
a tiny machine to fix inside her.
Then he painted her face, and made
some clothes for her. She was big
for a doll, as big as a real little girl.

"Now," said the wise man,
"I'll see if she can walk."
He stood the doll on the floor.
He started the tiny machine.
Slowly the doll moved her arms.
Stiffly she moved her legs.
Then she began to walk.
The wise man held her hand, and led her
round the room. She walked and walked
just like a real little girl.

"Now," said the wise man,
"I'll see if she can dance."

He pressed a tiny handle
in the machine.
Slowly the doll
moved her arms.
Stiffly she moved her legs.
Then she began to dance.
She danced and danced
just like a real little girl.

"She's pretty," said the wise man.
"She's clever, and as far as I know,
she's the first dancing doll
in the world."

The wise man took her to see
his friends. He held her hand, and she
walked along beside him.
People in the street had never thought
of such a thing as a doll
that could walk.

"Oh, look!" they said.
"The wise man has a little girl."

The wise man was very pleased
with his dancing doll, and he kept her

in his house for a long time.
Then he thought of one of his friends
who lived across the sea.

"My friend would be glad to see
such a wonderful doll," he thought.
"I'll go and stay with him,
and take the dancing doll."

The wise man packed his bag.
He put the doll in a large wooden box.
He nailed down the lid, and tied the box
tightly with strong rope. He wrote
his name on a label, and stuck it
on the box. Then he went on a ship,
and found his cabin. His bag and the box
with the doll in it were put on the deck
with other people's bags and boxes.
The captain gave the signal,
and the ship sailed away across the sea.

The sea was very rough,
and the wise man stayed in his cabin.
The waves splashed higher and higher.
The ship tossed up and down,

and the wise man's box,
and all the other bags and boxes
slid to and fro upon the deck.

Somehow all the tossing and the sliding
and the shaking of the box,
started the machine inside the wooden doll.
Slowly her arms began to move.
Stiffly her legs began to move.
But there was no room to walk inside
the box, and there was no room to dance.
So the doll's little hands
could only go tap, tap, tap on the lid,
and her little feet could only go bang,
bang, bang against the box.

Soon the sea became quiet
and calm again. The captain of the ship
went on deck to see if the bags
and the boxes were still safe.
To his surprise he heard,

"Tap, tap, tap."

What could it be?
There was no one there but himself.

He stood still and listened.
The boxes and bags
had stopped sliding about.
Nothing seemed to be moving.
Yet again the captain heard,

"Tap, tap, tap."

"What can it be?" he thought.
He went nearer, and looked among
the bags and the boxes.
He heard the sound again, louder now.

"Tap, tap, tap."

"It seems to be coming
from this box,"

he thought. "I'd better open it,
and see what's inside."
He untied the rope, and pulled
some nails from the lid with his knife.
Then he opened the box.

To his surprise he saw a doll.
It was made of wood, and was quite big,
—as big as a real little girl.
The captain was more puzzled
than before. Surely a doll couldn't
have gone tap, tap, tap inside the box!
He lifted her out, and stood her
on the deck for a moment.
She began to walk!
She walked and walked
just like a real little girl.
The captain could hardly believe his eyes.

Then the doll began to dance.
She danced and danced
just like a real little girl.

"Whoever heard of a doll
that could dance?" said the captain.

"I must be dreaming."

But the wooden doll went on dancing. The captain was afraid.

"It's magic," he thought. "I won't have a magic doll on my ship. I'll throw her into the sea."

And the captain caught hold of her and lifted her up, to throw her into the cold deep sea.

Luckily, at that very moment, the wise man came up on deck to see if his bag and the box were still safe. He was just in time to see the captain with the dancing doll.

"Stop, stop!" cried the wise man. "That doll is mine."

He ran across the deck and took the doll away from the captain.

"Your doll?" said the captain. "But it's magic! It walks and dances."

Then the wise man laughed, for he knew that the captain had been afraid. He told him how he had carved the doll from wood, and how he had made a tiny machine to put inside her.

"It isn't magic," he said. "It's the first dancing doll in the world."

"I'm sorry," said the captain. "Let me put her back in the box for you."

"No, no," said the wise man. "I think perhaps she'll be safer in my cabin with me."

So the dancing doll stayed with the wise man in his cabin, and she sailed across the sea after all.